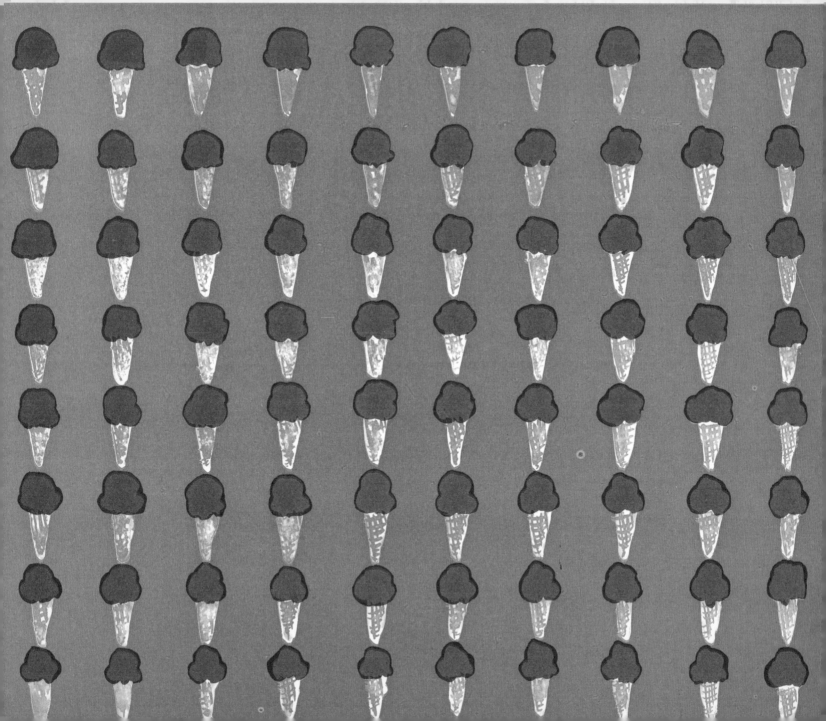

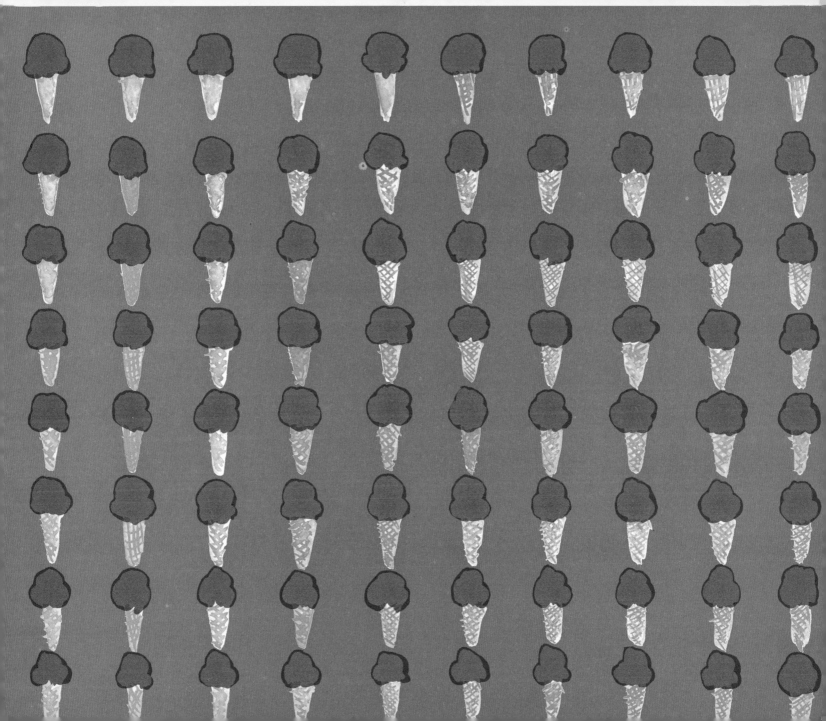

Holt, Rinehart and Winston   New York Chicago San Francisco

JOHN JOHN TWILLIGER

by William Wondriska

Holt Owlet Books is a paperback picture book series, carefully chosen for merit and popularity from a distinguished backlist of children's literature.

Owlet Titles You May Enjoy:

ALL IN THE MORNING EARLY by Sorche Nic Leodhas; illustrated by Evaline Ness
ALPHABET OF GIRLS by Leland Jacobs; illustrated by John E. Johnson
THE BEE-MAN OF ORN by Frank R. Stockton; illustrated by Maurice Sendak
A CERTAIN SMALL SHEPHERD by Rebecca Caudill; illustrated by William Pène du Bois
THE CIRCUS: A Book to Begin On by Mary Kay Phelan; illustrated by John Alcorn
COBWEB CASTLE by Jan Wahl; illustrated by Edward Gorey
COLL AND HIS WHITE PIG by Lloyd Alexander; illustrated by Evaline Ness
CONTRARY JENKINS by Rebecca Caudill and James Ayars; illustrated by Glen Rounds
EVAN'S CORNER by Elizabeth Starr Hill; illustrated by Nancy Grossman
JOHN JOHN TWILLIGER written and illustrated by William Wondriska
SAM, BANGS AND MOONSHINE written and illustrated by Evaline Ness
WHAT'S GOOD FOR A FOUR-YEAR-OLD? by William Cole; illustrated by Tomi Ungerer

for Ann

There once was a little town called Merryall.

In the middle of the town was the Big Hill.

At the top of the Big Hill was the Fort.

In the Fort was the Machine-Gun Man.

Merryall was the town of the Machine-Gun Man and the place where John John Twilliger and Fred the Dog lived.

But, as things turned out, the Machine-Gun Man was wrong. The people of Merryall went on obeying him, even when he got rid of the machine guns and turned the Fort into a Dance Palace with an enormous elevator that took fifty people at a time up from the town to the top of the Hill. This was partly because the people had got into the habit of obeying him and didn't care to change and partly because he made up a new set of rules. Since the rules were things like "Be friendly and others will befriend you" and "Every adult should have one pet and every child as many pets as he or she wants," people wanted to obey them.

John John Twilliger happened to be very good at doing things, the kind of things that are usually called getting into mischief. Once he found an old cannon and a pile of worn out gun belts in the Machine-Gun Man's rubbish heap at the foot of the Big Hill. He wrapped himself up in the gun belts so that only his bright red hair showed and rolled the cannon through the streets yelling, "Yah, yah, run if you can! Here I come, the Machine-Gun Man!"

Another time he climbed halfway up the Big Hill
and dropped balloons filled with paint as red as his hair
on the bell tower of the schoolhouse.

And, on a very hot day, he had gone swimming in
the pool around the statue of the Machine-Gun Man
that stood in the center of town.

Every single time John John Twilliger got punished so hard that he couldn't sit down for several days. But he could not stop wanting to do things. And the thing he liked to do best of all was dance. He tried a few steps as he went down the street, but dancing was no fun alone.

"Will you dance with me Mr. Woodman?" he asked when he met the woodcutter at the next corner.

"Dancing is against the rules," said the woodcutter angrily. "Now run home boy, before you get into any mischief. The Machine-Gun Man is watching."

At the next corner, John John Twilliger met Mrs. Wetneck carrying her laundry. "Will you dance with me, Mrs. Wetneck?"

Mrs. Wetneck looked fearfully up at the Big Hill. "Do you want me to break the rules? Now run home, boy, and quickly. The Machine-Gun Man is watching."

"No one's any fun," muttered John John Twilliger as he walked along the empty streets of Merryall. "They're all afraid to do anything."

He stared up at the Fort on the Big Hill. Then he quickly brought his eyes back to the street. Maybe the Machine-Gun Man *is* watching, thought John John Twilliger, but he won't see me if I dance with Fred the Dog in our secret place.

The secret place was a cave right under the Big Hill. Fred the Dog was John John Twilliger's biggest piece of mischief. For one thing, the Machine-Gun Man did not allow dogs in Merryall. For another, Fred the Dog was John John Twilliger's friend. So by keeping Fred the Dog in the cave and bringing him food and dancing with him John John Twilliger was breaking three rules.

Fred was a big lump of a dog with fur as red as John John's hair and a disposition happy enough to make anyone love him. John John Twilliger loved him most.

Whenever he could, he would sneak off to the cave and they would dance and dance and dance until they were nothing more than a red blur. But Fred the Dog also liked to explore, so John John had to keep him tied up in the cave which neither of them liked.

"Here I come, Fred," called John John softly when he got to the mouth of the cave. "Get ready for a good dance."

But there was nothing in the cave except a piece of broken rope.

All that hot day John John Twilliger searched Merryall, but there was no sign of Fred the Dog.

Finally he went wearily back to his own home. Sitting on the steps, watching the sun go down, he looked up the Big Hill at the Fort. That was the only place in Merryall he hadn't searched. John John Twilliger jumped off the steps. He knew where Fred the Dog must have gone.

It was twilight when John John Twilliger began the long climb up the Big Hill. By the time he reached the top, the moon had come up and was shining brightly. In the pale light, the walls of the Fort looked as high as the Big Hill itself. That silly dog couldn't climb over so he must have crawled under, thought John John Twilliger as he walked cautiously around the wall. There must be a hole in the wall somewhere that's big enough to let Fred the Dog in.

John John Twilliger searched and searched, but all he could find was a hole barely big enough to allow him to crawl through—which he did. The wall was so thick that it seemed more like a tunnel than a hole, and the crawling seemed to take a long, long time. But finally John John Twilliger came out in the courtyard of the Machine-Gun Man's Fort. In the moonlight he could see all kinds of guns. There were cannons of all shapes and sizes, rifles, pistols, revolvers, and—most of all—machine guns. John John Twilliger couldn't count them all.

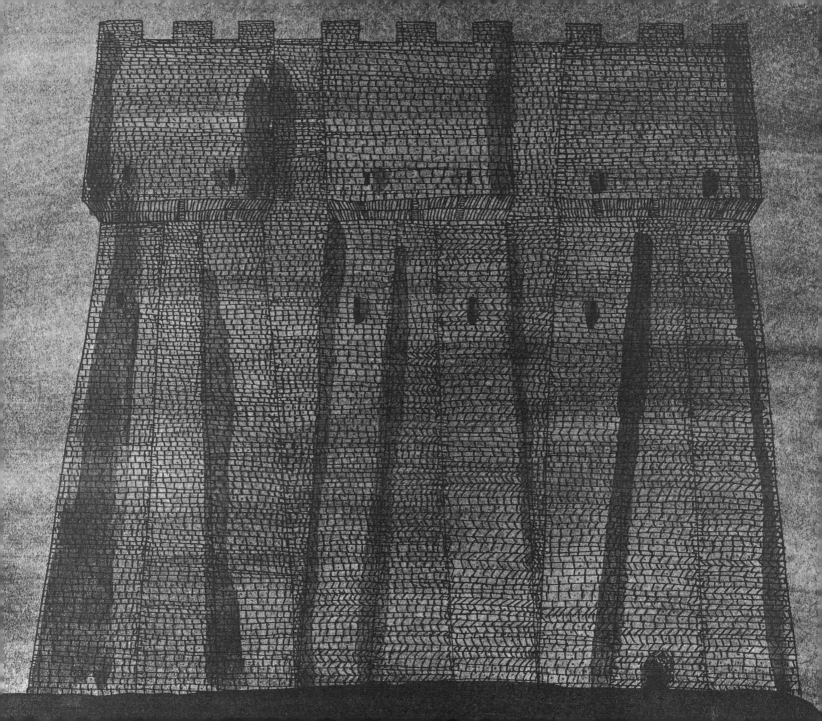

In fact, he didn't even try to count them, because just then a shadow moved behind the biggest cannon. John John Twilliger's red hair stood up on end. The shadow moved again and John John Twilliger's eyes bulged as he stared at it.

And then the shadow barked softly and everything was all right. John John Twilliger ran across the courtyard and hugged Fred the Dog and they both made lots of happy noises.

Then they set off to find the hole through which Fred the Dog had entered the Fort. John John Twilliger knew that Fred the Dog could never squeeze through the little tunnel he had used. But the moon had gone behind a cloud, and it was too dark to see. Suddenly Fred the Dog knocked over a machine gun with a very loud clatter.

John John Twilliger held his breath, but it was too late. There was a big click and floodlights went on, making the courtyard as bright as day.

"Come here, my pretties," said a horrible raspy voice. "I want to see who has dared to invade the Fort of the Machine-Gun Man."

John John Twilliger and Fred the Dog sort of pushed each other to the foot of the stairs they now saw leading down into the courtyard. At the head of the stairs stood the Machine-Gun Man. It was hard to tell if he *was* a man. He had so many gun belts twisted around his body that he was the shape of a fat box. A big helmet hid his face and on top of the helmet was a tiny machine gun. On his feet were huge black boots and in each hand he held a large machine gun.

"Did you think you could win without firing a shot?" asked the raspy voice. "How dare you invade without firing one shot?"

"Please, sir," said John John Twilliger, "we didn't invade. Fred the Dog was exploring, and I came to find him."

The helmet bent forward. "So that's a dog, is it? How dare he come here? Dogs are against the rules."

"He didn't know," explained John John Twilliger.

"But *you* knew," shouted the horrible voice, "and *you* invaded my fort! Why, why, why?"

"Fred the Dog is my friend," said John John Twilliger. "I had to come and get him out of trouble."

"What is a friend?" asked the Machine-Gun Man.

John John Twilliger didn't know quite how to explain. "Well, we dance together," he said finally.

"And what is dancing? Stop speaking in riddles."

"Dancing is something you—you do," stammered John John Twilliger.

"Show me," shouted the Machine-Gun Man. "Show me immediately!"

Poor John John Twilliger was so frightened by this time that he could hardly move. But somehow he moved his cold stiff feet and shaking legs into the first steps of a dance. Fred the Dog was not afraid because he didn't know any better, and when he saw the dance starting, he began to prance gaily. Around and around he went and soon John John Twilliger forgot to be afraid and was dancing too, faster and faster.

"Stop!" screamed the Machine-Gun Man. "I want to dance too."

So John John Twilliger tried to show him the basic steps, but the Machine-Gun Man was so weighted down with guns that he couldn't move. First he had to lay down his machine guns, and then, one by one, he started taking off the gun belts. But he was still clumsy.

"I *think*," said John John Twilliger, "that you can't see very well with your helmet on."

"No!" said the Machine-Gun Man, but quite softly. "I never take off my helmet. You see, all my life I have had to conceal my terrible hair. It's *red!*"

"So is mine and so is Fred the Dog's," pointed out John John Twilliger.

"True enough." The Machine-Gun Man sounded surprised. "Then you won't be able to tease me about having red hair." He took off his helmet, but he kept stumbling.

"It's your boots," John John Twilliger explained. "It's hard to dance in big boots."

"I can't take off my boots," the Machine-Gun Man whispered. "Not my boots. They make me tall. I'm really very small, you see, smaller than other men."

"Well, I'm small too," said John John Twilliger cheerfully.

"That is so." The Machine-Gun Man stared for a moment and then he sat down on the stairs. John John Twilliger helped him pull off his boots, and when the Machine-Gun Man stood up, they found he was three inches taller than John John Twilliger.

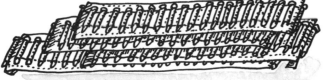

And then they danced—and danced—and danced until they were nothing more than a red blur, the three of them. And finally they fell down exhausted.

"You're a very good dancer," said John John Twilliger, when he got his breath back. "Why did you make a rule against it?"

"I couldn't bear to see people enjoying themselves. When I first came to Merryall, people *were* merry here —all but me. I was small and had red hair and no friends. So I built the Fort and then people had to obey me and my guns, and they stopped being merry."

"How would it be," suggested John John Twilliger, "if you were merry too? I mean Fred the Dog and I can be your friends and we'll have a lot of fun dancing. We *need* someone to dance with."

"Well," said the Machine-Gun Man cautiously, "we can try it. Why don't you come again tomorrow night? But, mind you, this is our secret. I don't want the people to stop obeying my rules—and they might, if they knew the truth about me.

But, as things turned out, the Machine-Gun Man was wrong. The people of Merryall went on obeying him, even when he got rid of the machine guns and turned the Fort into a Dance Palace with an enormous elevator that took fifty people at a time up from the town to the top of the Hill. This was partly because the people had got into the habit of obeying him and didn't care to change and partly because he made up a new set of rules. Since the rules were things like "Be friendly and others will befriend you" and "Every adult should have one pet and every child as many pets as he or she wants," people wanted to obey them.

A very popular rule was: "On Midsummer Eve there will be a Dance Festival and the Best Dancer will get free ice cream every day for a year." The Mayor (formerly the Machine-Gun Man) always tied for first place with John John Twilliger and they split the prize. Fred the Dog came in second, but he didn't care, since the Mayor and John John Twilliger always shared their ice cream with him anyway.

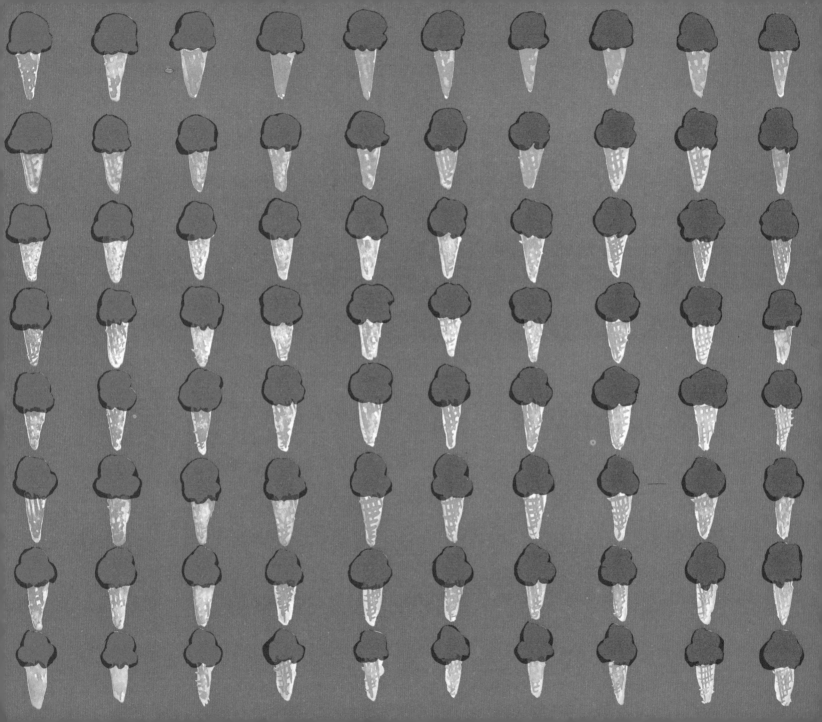

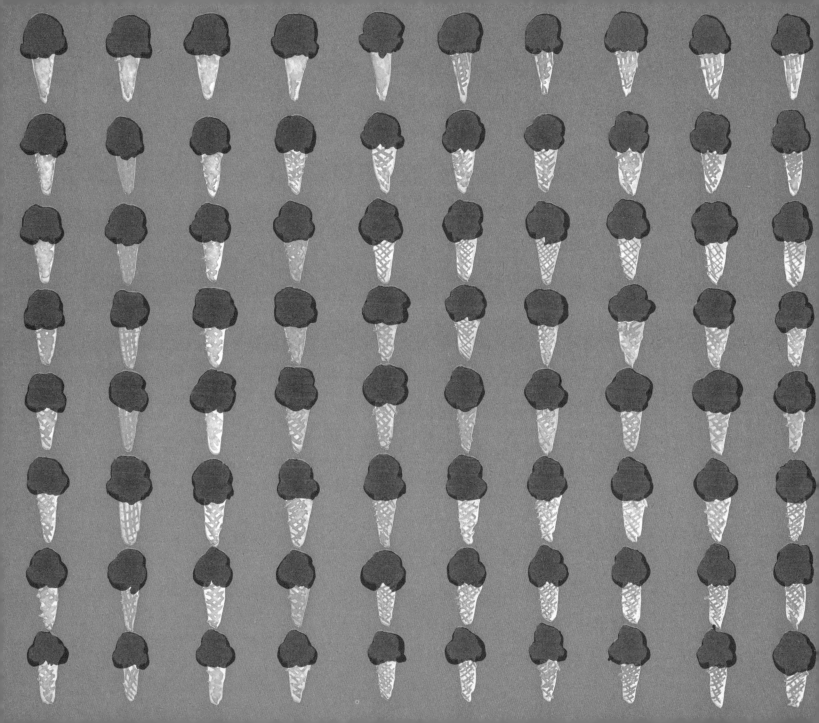